This Book Belongs To:

_____

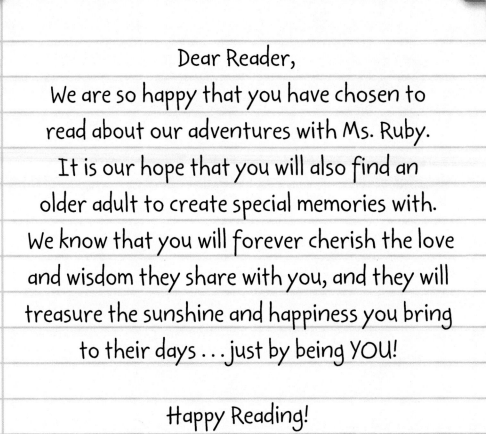

Dear Reader,
We are so happy that you have chosen to
read about our adventures with Ms. Ruby.
It is our hope that you will also find an
older adult to create special memories with.
We know that you will forever cherish the love
and wisdom they share with you, and they will
treasure the sunshine and happiness you bring
to their days . . . just by being YOU!

Happy Reading!
Xoxo,
The Gigi Squad

Ms. Ruby
and the
GIGI SQUAD

Friendship
Comes in All Ages

Written By

Vickie Rodgers

Illustrated By

Vidya Valsudevan

Meet Ms. Ruby.

She's a fun-loving lady who is 93 years old. Lately she has been feeling a bit sad.

One day Ms. Ruby
called Gigi.

"Gigi,"
Ms. Ruby said,
"I miss spending time
with children.
They always bring
sunshine and happiness
everywhere they go."

Gigi knew just what to do!
She decided to bring the
Gigi Squad to meet Ms. Ruby.

What's the Gigi Squad?
It's a group of kind-hearted kids who
happen to be Gigi's grandchildren:
Avery, Caroline,
Cole, and Will.

GIGI SQUAD

Gigi gathered the squad.

"Kids," she said, "how would you
like to visit my friend, Ms. Ruby?
She was once a nurse just like me.
She sometimes feels lonely,
and is wishing for visitors."

"Where does she live?"
asked Avery.

"Did she take care of sick people?"
asked Cole.

"Why is she lonely?"
asked Caroline.

"What if she doesn't like us?"
asked Will.

Gigi answered all of their questions:
"Ms. Ruby lives at
Friendship Village Care Center,
which is a home for older people.

She was a nurse for a long time
and has cared for many people.

She doesn't have any grandchildren
and sometimes that makes her feel
lonely, and, of course she will like
you— you will all bring so much
happiness into her life, and she will
add friendship and joy to yours."

"What is it like to visit a care center?"
asked Will.

Gigi explained that they might see some people sitting in special chairs that have wheels to help them get from place to place. Some people may be using equipment to help them walk.

"One thing is for sure ... They all love children."

The kids were a bit nervous about meeting Ms. Ruby
for the first time, but Ms. Ruby's big smile and the
sparkle in her eyes let them know how happy she was
to see them. They chuckled at the stories that she told
them about the fun things she did in her childhood.

On the way home, the squad decided that since Ms. Ruby can't get out to see the world, maybe they could bring some sunshine into her world.

They also agreed that it would be nice to meet the other residents at the care center.

"I have an idea!"
shouted Caroline.
"Let's plan some fun days
for Ms. Ruby!"

"Yes!"
they all shouted.

"First, let's give her a
surprise birthday party,"
said Avery.

"Ms. Ruby's birthday
is next week,"
Grandma Gigi said,
"so we'd better get busy."

The planning began.

"I'll help bake the cake,"
said Caroline.

"I'll carry the balloons,"
said Will.

"I'll hold the flowers and the
party decorations,"
said Avery.

"I'll carry the gift,"
said Cole.

The kids went to see Ms. Ruby, and when she opened the door, they shouted:

SURPRISE!!

Avery played Happy Birthday
on the piano, and
the Gigi Squad sang.

"This is the best party
I've ever had,"
said Ms. Ruby.
"You bring me so much joy!"

"I have an idea for another
special day for Ms. Ruby,"
said Avery.
"I'm going to invite her to my middle school musical.
Ms. Ruby will love that and, after all, I do have a lead part."

Before the musical started,
Avery introduced Ms. Ruby
to her theater friends.
"This is my new friend,"
Avery announced.

Gigi and Ms. Ruby smiled as they
watched Avery's performance.

"This has been a special night,"
Ms. Ruby said
when the play ended.

Middle School
Musical

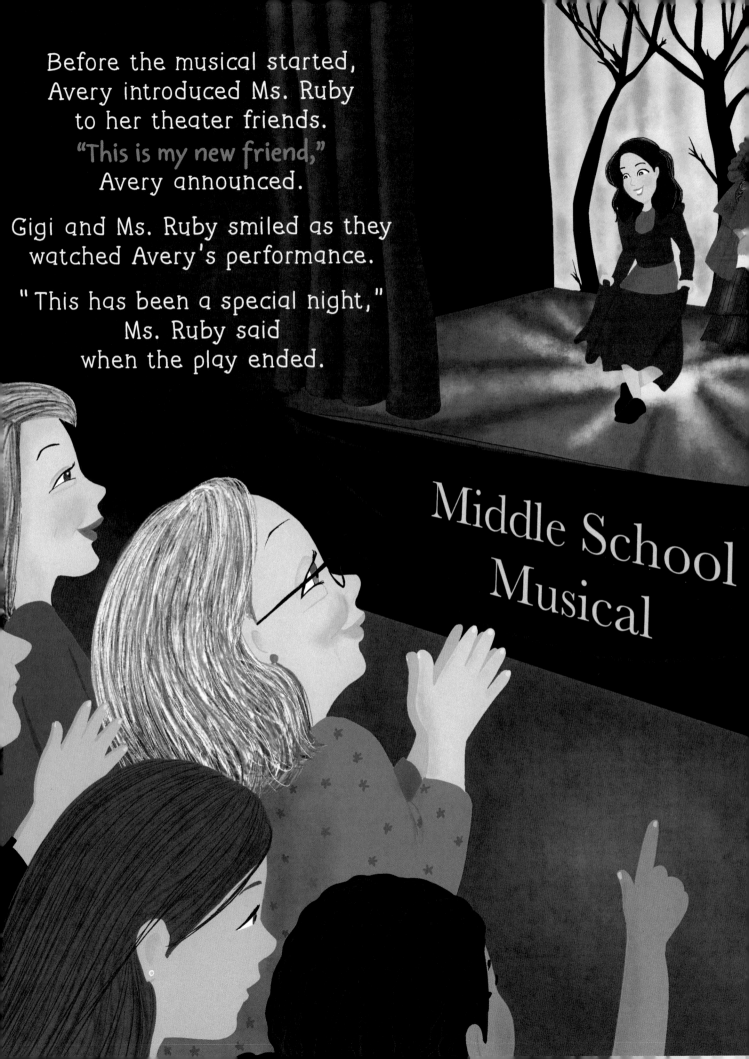

"I choose next,"
Caroline said.
"I want to have a tea party
with Ms. Ruby!"

Gigi helped Caroline make the tea and set the table with
Ms. Ruby's pretty cups and saucers.
They spent the afternoon eating cake, drinking tea
and telling each other stories.
"I feel just like a grownup,"
said Caroline,
carefully sipping her tea.

Ms. Ruby loved everything
about the tea party.
"Thank you, Caroline,"
she said,
"This has been
a tea party I will
always remember."

"I choose Halloween!"
said Cole.
"No, I choose Halloween!"
said Will.

"Let's both do Halloween!"
they said together.
"Done!"

Friendship Village

Care Center

Police

LWNORDR

On Halloween night, Cole and Will arrived at
Friendship Village Care Center.

They paraded around, saying trick or treat to everyone and handed out special treats to all.

Ms. Ruby and the other residents loved the parade.
"You made everyone so happy," said Ms. Ruby.
"Bringing sunshine to you is fun,"
said Will.

"What can we do next to bring more sunshine and happiness to Ms. Ruby?" asked Caroline.

"I know!" said Avery, "Let's decorate a bag and fill it with treats. We can call it THE SUNSHINE BAG!"

On their next visit, the squad proudly handed Ms. Ruby the SUNSHINE BAG.

"Thank you for the wonderful gift!" she said.

Christmas
was coming soon!

The kids were thinking of unusual ways to make their first Christmas with Ms. Ruby an exciting event.

Gigi took the squad shopping to get party supplies.
They bought a small tree for Ms. Ruby's room, and
each kid chose a meaningful ornament. They picked
out a colorful stocking and filled it with goodies.

Then they made Ms. Ruby a one-of-a-kind necklace.
They each stamped their names on metal circles and
then created a small heart with the words

Bonus Grandma

in the center.

The children were so excited to decorate Ms. Ruby's room for the holidays!

"What a lovely surprise," Ms. Ruby exclaimed. "I haven't had a Christmas tree for many years."

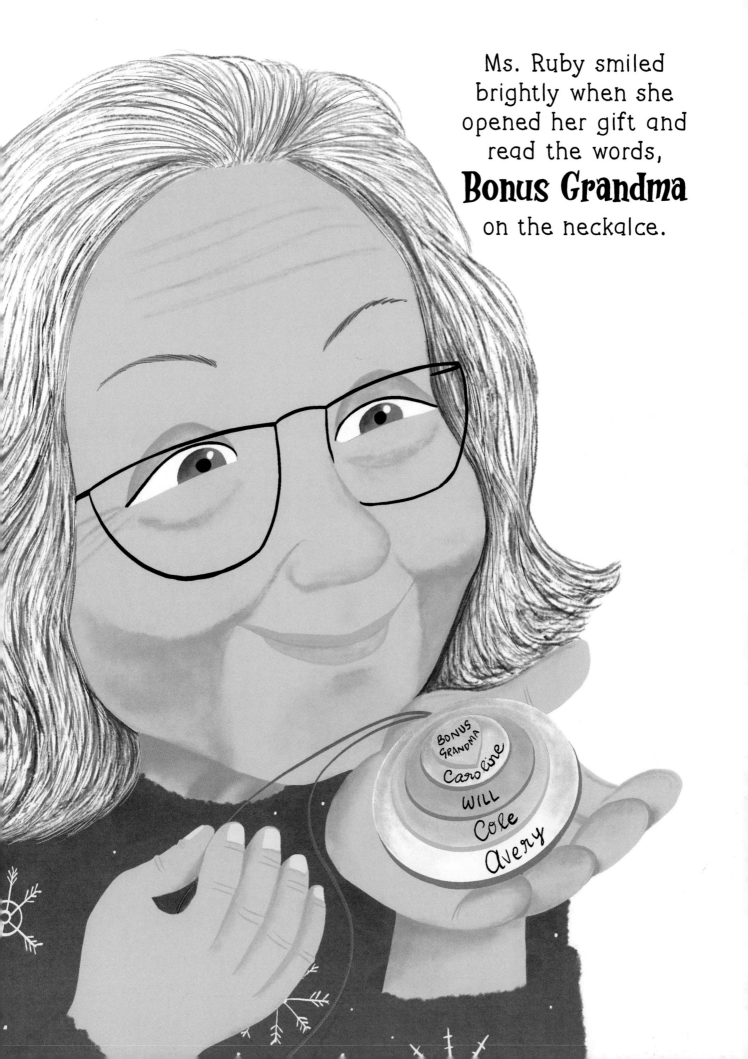

Ms. Ruby smiled brightly when she opened her gift and read the words, **Bonus Grandma** on the neckalce.

"Everyone needs a **Bonus Grandma**
like Ms. Ruby to share
their wisdom and bring
them joy," Gigi said.

"Plus, lots of older people need kids like us to make memories and share their sunshiny days," said Avery. Caroline, Cole, and Will nodded as the members of **THE GIGI SQUAD** began planning their next adventure with Ms. Ruby.

Discussion Questions

1. Do you know an older person in your family, a friend's family, or your neighborhood?

2. If so, have you ever spent time with this person getting to know them?

3. What was your favorite activity that the Gigi Squad did with Ms. Ruby?

4. What other activities can you think of to do with an older person?

Where,
oh where
can YOU
find a
Special Elderly Friend?

Under a rock?

No, silly!

In your house attic?

In a doghouse?

We hope not!

Probably not!

In your Neighborhood?

At your church?

Maybe!

Most certainly!

In a local Retirement Home?

Absolutely yes!

Kindness Projects

Project #1: The Memory Making Project

During one of your visits with your new older adult friend:

1. Choose some questions from the below list to ask your new friend.
2. Write their answers down for later.
3. Create a booklet of pictures that you draw based on their answers.
4. Give them the gift of your colorful and creative Memory Booklet.

Possible Questions to Ask:

- Who was your favorite teacher and why?
- What was your favorite subject in school?
- Did you ever play a musical instrument?
- What is your favorite music?
- What was your home like as a child?
- What were holidays like growing up?
- Did you have any pets?
- Do you have any favorite foods?
- Do you have a hobby?
- Did you have any sisters and brothers? If so, what were your siblings' names?
- What is your most cherished family tradition?
- Do you have children? If so, what is your favorite story about each of them?
- Who are three people in history that you admire most and why?

Project #2: The Sunshine Bag Project

1. Create your own Sunshine Bag.
2. Fill your bag with special treasures that your new friend would like.
3. With a parent's help, deliver the SUNSHINE BAG to your new friend.
4. Ask your parents to share a photo of your sunshine bag and treasures to "The Sunshine Bag Project" Facebook Page.

Things You Can Include in your Sunshine Bag:

- Adult Coloring Book
- Puzzle Books
- Coloring Supplies
- Ink Pens/Pencils
- Paint by Number Set
- Craft Kits
- Jigsaw Puzzles
- Stationary, Envelopes, and Stamps
- Artificial Flowers
- Photo Frames
- Eyeglass Cleaning Cloths
- Magnifying Glass
- Nail Care Kits
- Shave Gel/Cream
- Lotion
- Lip Balm
- Comb and Brush Set
- Jewelry
- Magazines
- Calendar
- Personalized Coffee Mug
- Cozy and Soft Blanket
- Cozy Gripper Socks
- House Shoes (Non-Skid)
- Neck Pillow
- Favorite Snacks (Ms. Ruby Loves Dark Chocolate)
- Packets of Cocoa
- Fresh Fruit
- Bags of Pre-Popped Popcorn
- Cookies
- Throw Pillow for Bed with Positive Saying

Ruby Foster, also known as Ms. Ruby, is a 93 year-old former World War II United States Cadet Nurse. She and Vickie have shared many adventures. Ruby was the first Cadet Nurse in the U.S. to be honored by a trip to Washington, DC aboard the Greater St. Louis Honor Flight. Vickie accompanied her for what turned out to be a major highlight of both of their lives. Ms. Ruby is presently living her best life in a caring retirement community. She has loved every visit and fun-filled adventure the Gigi Squad has created for her.

Avery is 15 years old and is active in her high school theater and choir groups. She has performed in several musicals and can be found riding horses in her spare time. She loves music and is a talented piano player with a gift for learning new songs. Avery lives with her mom, dad, and ten-year-old brother, Will. They have two dogs, Toby and Snickers. Avery has enjoyed her time making lasting memories with Ms. Ruby.

Caroline is 12 years old and is active in volleyball and swimming. She loves to listen to music and also enjoys helping her mom with a local charitable organization. Caroline is a great student and always strives to do her best. She lives with her mom, dad, and ten-year-old brother, Cole. They have two boxer dogs, Ali and Tiger. Caroline has also loved creating memories for Ms. Ruby and spending time with her.

Cole is ten years old and loves to play both ice hockey and street hockey. He loves watching hockey games with his family and enjoys swimming in his spare time. Cole lives with his mom, dad, and twelve-year-old sister, Caroline. He and Caroline love to play with their dogs, Ali and Tiger. Cole has had a great time bringing joy to Ms. Ruby and has created some special cards and hand-drawn pictures for her to cherish.

Will is ten years old and loves to play both ice hockey and street hockey. He and Cole spend a lot of time on the ice together and share a special bond. He also enjoys swimming and playing video games. Will has the deepest dimples, which always brings a smile to Ms. Ruby's face. He lives with his mom, dad, fifteen-year-old sister Avery, and their dogs, Toby and Snickers. Will has also enjoyed his time with Ms. Ruby.

Vickie Rodgers is a former Professor of Nursing Education, and is presently the Clinical Educator of a large retirement community. She has a passion for working with the elderly, and creating this book is her bucket-list labor of love. Vickie's goal is to help children realize that older adults can bring love into their lives, along with valuable lessons. Watching her grandchildren bring sunshine to the real-life Ms. Ruby has brought joy to Vickie and her family. She and her husband have three grown children, four grandchildren, and two goldendoodles.

About the Illustrator

Vidya Vasudevan has been a children's book illustrator for over 16 years, and enjoys bringing ideas and visions to life through her illustrations. In her process, Vidya explores different styles and media that goes with each unique story. She draws inspiration from the diverse cultures of countries where she grew up. Vidya is a post-graduate in English literature, and her work background also involves being a layout artist at an animation studio and an enrichment teacher. She is now happy to bring together her love for children, literature and art as she illustrates, writes, and teaches.

Dedication

This book is dedicated to:

• Avery, Caroline, Cole, and Will, my amazing real life Gigi Squad. And to our sweet bonus granddaughter, Kristen. I am so proud of all of you and your kind and compassionate hearts. May you always be the sunshine in other's lives as you are in mine.

• Ruby, my forever BFF, fellow nurse, beautiful soul and Bonus Grandma to my Gigi Squad. May you always know how special you are to all of us.

• My Husband Bill who has traveled this new author journey with me every step of the way and been my biggest supporter

• My dream team without whom this journey could not have been possible April Cox (Mentor), Sarah Kathryn Frey (Designer extraordinaire, Mentor, and friend), Bobbie Hinman (Editor), and Linda Snyder (photographer).

• All of the precious older adults who are wishing for a friend and the amazing children who can bring them sunshine and happiness.

Publisher's Cataloging-in-Publication data

Names: Rodgers, Vickie, author. | Valsudevan, Vidya, illustrator.
Title: Ms. Ruby and the Gigi squad : friendship comes in all ages / written by Vickie Rodgers ; illustrated
by Vidya Valsudevan.
Description: Moro, IL: Cozy Doodle Publishing, 2021. | Summary: Four children known as the Gigi Squad befriend a
delightful ninety-two year old lady named Ms. Ruby. Ms. Ruby lives in a care center for older
adults. The Gigi Squad steps into bring her sunshine and happiness with their visits.
Identifiers: LCCN: 2021917877 | ISBN: 978-1-7376713-0-5 (hardcover) | 978-1-7376713-1-2 (paperback)
| 978-1-7376713-2-9 (ebook)
Subjects: LCSH Older people--Care-- Juvenile literature. | Friendship-- Juvenile literature. | Family--
Juvenile literature. | CYAC Older people--Care. | Friendship. | Family. | BISAC JUVENILE NONFICTION /
Family / Multigenerational | JUVENILE NONFICTION / Social Topics / Friendship
Classification: LCC HV1451 .R63 2021 | DDC 362.6--dc23

THE SUNSHINE BAG

xoxo, The Gigi Squad

Made in the USA
Monee, IL
08 November 2021

Made in the USA
Monee, IL
08 November 2021